D0646252

T2-BUM-433

A Small Thing... but Big

Tony Johnston

Pictures by
Hadley Hooper

A NEAL PORTER BOOK
ROARING BROOK PRESS
NEW YORK

For Palo and Starly
—T. J.

Dedicated to Madeleine Sans Mouton Hooper-Graham,
the best mutt ambassador ever
—H.H.

A Neal Porter Book
Published by Roaring Brook Press
Roaring Brook Press is a division of Holtzbrinck Publishing Holdings Limited Partnership
175 Fifth Avenue, New York, New York 10010
The art for this book was created using a combination of relief printmaking and digital techniques.

mackids.com

Library of Congress Cataloging-in-Publication Data

Names: Johnston, Tony, 1942– author. | Hooper, Hadley, illustrator.
Title: A small thing . . . but big / Tony Johnston ; illustrated by Hadley Hooper.
Description: First edition. | New York : Roaring Brook Press, 2016. | "A Neal Porter Book." | Summary: Lizzie meets an elderly man and his companion, Cecile, at the park, but Lizzie is afraid of dogs, so she relies on her new friend to help her take things one step at a time.
Identifiers: LCCN 2015042626 | ISBN 9781626722569 (hardback)
Subjects: | CYAC: Self-confidence—Fiction. | Human-animal relationships—Fiction. | Dogs—Fiction. | Older people—Fiction. | Friendship—Fiction. | BISAC: JUVENILE FICTION / Animals / Dogs. | JUVENILE FICTION / Social Issues / Friendship. | JUVENILE FICTION / Social Issues / New Experience.
Classification: LCC PZ7.J6478 Slm 2016 | DDC [E]—dc23
LC record available at https://lccn.loc.gov/2015042626

Our books may be purchased in bulk for promotional, educational, or business use. Please contact your local bookseller or the Macmillan Corporate and Premium Sales Department at (800) 221-7945 ext. 5442 or by e-mail at MacmillanSpecialMarkets@macmillan.com
First edition 2016
Printed in China by Toppan Leefung Printing Ltd., Dongguan City, Guangdong Province

1 3 5 7 9 10 8 6 4 2

Lizzie went to the park.

She played, *tra-la-la.*

She ran, *zoom-zoom-zoom.*

She ran close to a dog.

Lizzie froze.

"Do not be worried," said the old man of the dog timidly.

"Does she bark?" asked Lizzie with worry anyway.

“Not at little children,”
said the old man.

"Does she bite?" asked Lizzie anxiously.

"Only her food," said the old man,
a bit anxious also, but with sparkle.

"Go ahead, give Cecile a pat."

Feeling reassured, carefully,
oh carefully, Lizzie patted Cecile.

Cecile sat soft and still.
She seemed to enjoy
those pattings.

“I patted a dog,” Lizzie said quietly.

“A small thing, but big,” said the old man, quietly too.

“Shall we walk Cecile?” he ventured in his quiet way.

GELATO

Lizzie felt uneasy.

"Do not be worried," said the old man.
"Cecile will *adore* walking with a child."

"She is quite adoring being with you," the old man said shyly.

"How springingly she walks."

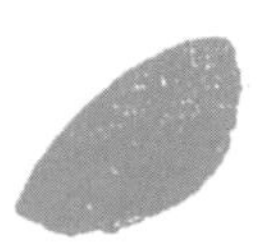

Lizzie walked springingly too.

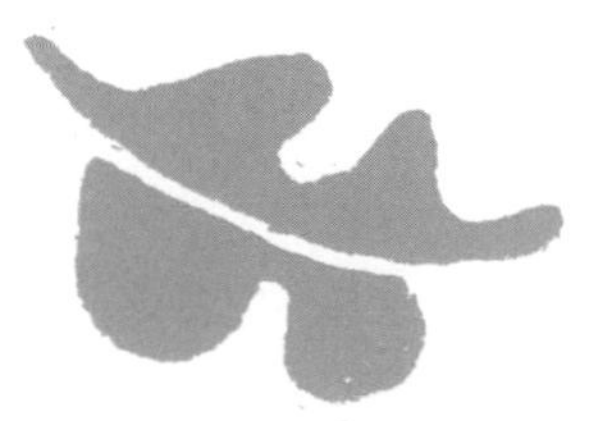

Walking with
a dog.

“She is a good dog,”
Lizzie said, patting Cecile.

A small thing, but big.

"All dogs are good
if you give them
a chance."

"Would you like
to hold her leash?"

"How?" asked Lizzie,
a little fearful.

"Just so."

Lizzie held the leash,
just so. And she and
the quiet old man
and the quiet dog,
Cecile, walked
quietly around
the park.

A small thing, but big.

"You know," ventured the old man,
"I believe you could take a little
walk with Cecile by yourself."

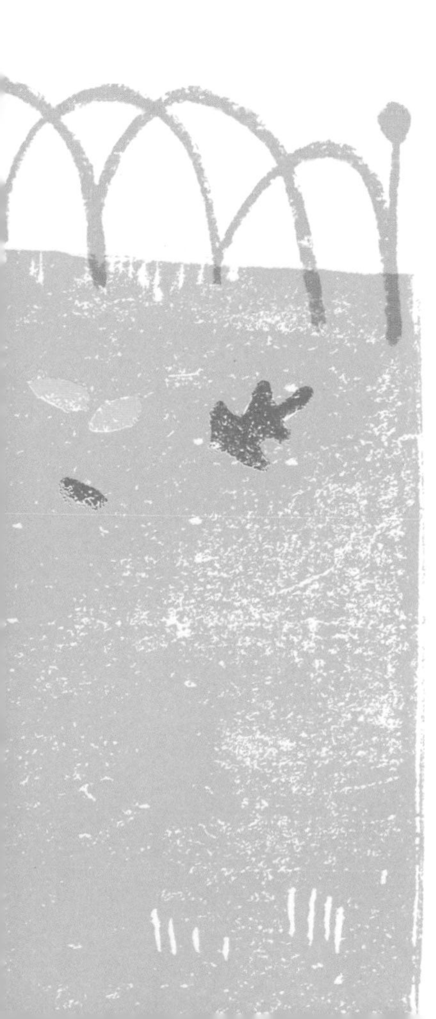

"I could?"

"You could."

Lizzie and Cecile walked
around the park.

Hesitant at first, then
springingly, oh springingly,

while the old man
watched from a bench.

Walking a dog alone.

A small thing, but big.

"I walked Cecile!"
said Lizzie, aglow.

"Magnificently,"
said the old man, aglow as well.

"Before today, I was very afraid of dogs,"
Lizzie told him.

The quiet old man replied,
"Before today, I was very afraid
of children."